Slime & Crime

The critics have spoken...

Michèle Laframboise

Slime & Crime

From the GGPD Files

Echofictions

A WOW Story

Original publication in Fiction River 22, 2017

Cover design by Echofictions
Cover pictures of snail © Shutterstock
Author portrait © Gilles Gagnon
Interior illustrations by the author

This book published by : Echofictions
Mississauga, Ontario

www.echofictions.com

ISBN 978-1-988339-67-2 (print)

Table of Contents

For Josette

who loves gardens,

cats and mysteries!

Slime & Crime

"I DIDN'T SEE A THING."

Melizz's skin was a riot of wrinkles and folds. Creamy sweat beads dribbled down his body, ending in a sticky puddle. He would have to shift his weight soon.

I shifted myself away from the witness, then opened my scent channels to assess his signed words. I smelled his sweat: neutral, devoid of the tang coming from badly metabolized water.

Liars couldn't help retaining their water.

Keeping more water inside meant the body's sweat would be saturated with salts. Droplets with high levels of salt induced an oxidation of the lipid complexes that maintained the skin's optimal elasticity.

Sweat told a lot about a slogger's dispositions. I had learned to minimize my own output to better smell others'. This particular skill gave me the best crime solving rate of the GGPD.

Most investigators concentrated on the slime trail.

Alas, this case could be a career-stopper. A strong scent of aster pods suffused the crime-scene, a bare sun-kissed granite rock, so much that a liar's sweat could get unnoticed.

I regretted not ordering Zgouish to get rid of the horrid, spiky pods. Those big sun-petaled umbrellas were annoying enough, without having to deal with their pods. Besides being spicy junk food, their scent messed with ambient smells.

But Zgouish was busy interrogating another witness. This one was a first-cycler, not even named yet. He was the one who found the desiccated body. Melizz had sent the olfactive call.

From my position, I could only glimpse a pale, slim eyestalk behind my partner's squat mass. His sheer size made Zgouish very apt at drawing information. His scarred shell was intimidating.

The witness' eyestalk was waving up and down, a sign of panic or of an urgent need to shift.

Excellent.

I left Zgouish working the witness and oozed back to the body.

The crime scene technician had finished sampling the tissues and the blood, but there was a hitch for the sweat.

Because of the afternoon discovery, the victim's skin had had time to dry, so there wasn't enough sweat left to smell out his last moments. Even the tell-tale slime trail had mostly evaporated.

It didn't bode well for the investigation.

"What do we have here?" I signed.

The technician's left eyestalk hovered about his evidence bag. Hardened brown pieces were floating in the semitransparent membrane.

"Not much to go. This hot spell has dried up the sweat."

He shrugged, sending ripples through his sides, in a two-four frequency wave. The dual frequency betrayed his annoyance, which had two causes.

First, there would be scant evidence to prove a murder, and much less to identify the perp. So he was wasting a perfectly good mid-afternoon.

Second, despite my being considered an unusual talent in the service, he was annoyed at being ordered around by an egg-sack. Of course, he couldn't express his discomfort, because the "egg-sack" was also the GGPD chief investigator.

*

As Zgouish and I slimed back to the GGPD headquarters, a sickly stench of corruption disturbed our familiar scent landscape. Sniffing a danger or a trap, I signaled to my partner to keep his stalks open.

"Take care," he signed back.

I inched along the path, tension racking my nerves. I could retract in my shell almost instantly, but that knowledge didn't help. A shell gave some sloggers a false sense of security.

A grey furred wall blocked the path. I retracted my stalks: it was positively stinking.

Zgouish undulated to a small erect branch and slimed up it. Then, his powerful foot and sides clinging to the branch, he extended his torso.

"It's a mouse," he signed. "Dead."

"Any wounds?"

"Marks on the neck. A deathclaw, I think."

I contracted in fear, grateful that Zgouish had turned his eyestalks toward the dead mouse.

Most deathclaws ignored us, because of our hard shell. But the flying ones could lift a slogger and crash his shell by letting it fall from a tree's height. Hence our age-old habit of treading undercover.

This was why Glam's body location made no sense. No slogger in his right mind would let himself bake in the midday sun.

*

THE GGPD OCCUPIED AN OLD BURROW under a dying maple tree, a short distance from a yummy cabbage patch. Already, alderbrush saplings were moving in for the kill, their ruthless roots obstructing underground passages.

The place needed maintenance, but the burrow's last owner had had a fateful encounter with Black Death.

When Big Thumper disappeared, Zgouish and I followed his warm furry scent to the northern limit of Garden. We found his mangled remains at the edge of the Grey Plains, crushed against the cliff upon which we stood. Only his pair of long vibration captors were recognizable.

Big Thumper's death saddened us all. Since then, a new family occupied the premises.

I extended my lower stalks, wary for furry smells. Rabbits usually left us alone, but their excitable cubs were another story. Fortunately, there were less of those around, as various deathclaws had feasted on the more stupid.

(Which was: most of them.)

The GGPD entrance was a smaller corridor from the main passage. The technician oozed back to his lab, the desiccated remains glued to his shell.

I passed under a hairy alder root to the Chief's chamber.

The place smelled of a practical mind. Meaning, gastropod comfort before function.

From a recess in the left-stalk wall wafted aromas of cabbage fragments and, yes, yummy strawberries! A faint light source came from a hollowed-out root (an informant's access).

The first thing you noticed about the Greater Garden Police Department Chief was his gigantic shell. The patterns, which would have been yellow and purple, were almost rubbed out by dozens of scars. His right eyestalk was a stump.

A survivor of the Southern Cabbage Patch Wars, The Chief was pushing seven cycles, a prodigious feat of longevity. So his wisdom was sought after, sloggers even coming from the neighboring jurisdictions.

I delivered my report, trying not to look at the pale termites crawling from the woodworks.

As the tech had guessed, the Chief was not convinced.

"Could be a natural death," he said, his short sensory stalks popping up and down.

It happened all the time: some stupid first-cycler would feast too long on yummy leaves, then doze off in an exposed place, unaware of the rising heat. He would wake in the sun, to find out that his body's water reserves were already spent.

But the deceased was an old foot in Garden, a four-cycler.

"No way the vic would have laid down for a nap in an exposed surface," I said.

"Glam knew better than that," Zgouish added.

The Chief moved his remaining eyestalk in a circular pattern.

"I guess. You said there was a large amount of dry aster pods on the slab? They may hide something else. Gowoon, talk to this Merviz again. Ask him about the pods."

I oozed back, leaving a trail of shame. I knew there was something amiss!

*

THE MID-AFTERNOON was slogging toward late afternoon when we convened in a nice secluded space in southern Garden.

We found Melizz's shell easy enough, by his mucus smell. I rounded the shell, mentally rehearsing my interrogation.

And stopped in my slime trail. A hard creamy wall blocked the shell. Nasty. We would have to go through our witness' calcareous epiphragm layer to get at him.

"Zgouish?" I signed.

My partner erected himself up, then fell over the closed door. He chewed and chewed, until his efforts paid off. Zgouish ripped through the epiphragm like it was wasp's paper.

Then, to my surprise, he reeled back from the shell like it was made of copper. My lower stalks captured my partner's olfactive emission, an explicit expletive.

Worm shit.

I stretched an eyestalk inside.

The shell was packed with brown spheres the size of eggs. A powerful, lingering smell wafted from it. It was a mix of yeast and honey, a very sought-after drug.

I sniffed as hard as I could, but the sector was bare of useful clues.

*

Ya think a deathclaw got him? Zgouish asked, green leafy shreds hanging from his mouth.

We were eating under a veined cabbage leaf, discussing our investigation. The weather was perfect, and none of us was in a particular hurry to report back our findings (or the lack of those) to the Chief.

"Melizz wouldn't have time to seal the shell."

And a four-cycler like Melizz wouldn't fall prey to a deathclaw.

"How did he manage to get an extra shell?" I asked.

Zgouish extended his massive body to grab a leaf's edge. The move exposed his sexy, meandering lower lip and his flat underside. I directed my eyestalks to the packed earth.

My partner made me feel light-footed, sometimes.

"Oldest ruse in the book," he signed. "He pilfered a similar-looking shell from some deathclaws' pile of refuse, and sealed it using his own mucus."

"He had been using that extra shell for a while," I said. "Because he left a nice stash of yeast inside. Which re-minded me. Why did you jump away from it?"

My partner's lower stalks twisted uneasily.

"I don't touch the stuff. The yeast, I mean."

"Why?"

He moved his sensory stalks in a circle. When he was content no snails or slug could scent or see our conversation, he continued, keeping his emissions as low as he could.

"When I was barely out of the egg, I went with my brothers foraging around Back Door—"

"Hey!" I emitted. "It's prohibited to go there. All first-cyclers are warned about Back Door Area."

He shrugged, a bad-slogger move so appealing that I almost forgot my question.

"We were as stupid as those rabbit-cubs. We went following each other's slime in the Area, when we smelled the most attractive aroma ever. It came from a glittering, golden lake.

"Beer," I said, in a deadly scent tone.

"I had a good sight already, so I noticed the lake edges, round as the full moon. My foremost brother plunged in."

He paused. An acidic odor of shame rose from his sides.

"I hate to admit it, but I was curious. So I tasted the stuff, from the edge. It was the most marvellous taste, ever. It invaded my brain like a parasite, wanting more."

"And?"

"I plunged and drank so much that I felt dizzy. All scents got mingled. Then I couldn't smell my bros. I felt their soft shells under my foot. They were not moving anymore!"

The Chief had campaigned hard to educate the population about beer traps.

"So I tried to get out, to no avail. When I felt my lung about to explode, a giant lifted the lake —it was a round recipient— and poured it in a dark plastic container. The giant put a lid on the container and lifted it. It landed on a hard surface, shaking the plastic wall.

"I slimed up to the lid, finding no way out. Later, a deep vibration hammered through my shell. The lid opened in a flash of blinding light. The container tilted, so the earth, the beer, my brothers' corpses were flung into a bigger maw."

"And you?"

"I was still on the lid; an abrupt move shook me free. I found myself on the grey plain, my shell cracked."

"The North Grey Plain?"

He munched steadily.

"I slogged on the hard surface. I was hurting all over. A powerful vibration passed through my foot. I twisted my eyes and that was when I saw them."

"Them?"

"Black death. They roamed the Grey Plain."

Curiosity was gobbling me up.

"How do they look?" I asked.

"Like a giant black foot wrapped around a silver shell."

"Do they leave a slime trail?"

"No. They smell like a mix of rubber, iron, copper."

I almost choked on my mouthful of green. Copper was the nastiest metal you could imagine in Garden.

"They roll fast, like a seed pod pushed by a brisk wind. They go in groups of two or four. I don't think even the biggest deathclaws could hurt them."

He paused, munching more of the leaf.

"So this is why you turn down Basement assignments."

"I cannot be around beer."

I steered the conversation away.

"That mouse we found. Why did the deathclaw leave the body intact?"

"Maybe a furry one? They're known to leave their prey uneaten."

Furry deathclaws. We would pick their musky scent near Back Door Area or the cabbage patch, or glimpse a confusion of grey and black fur.

Zgouish's attitude relaxed with the change of subject.

"You would think that, equipped with those earth-digging claws, mice could defend themselves."

"Mice have tiny claws. Worms told me that walking deathclaws were huge."

Zgouish stopped eating, his left eyestalk jerking up and down.

"What?" I enquired.

"Worms. You still frequent those things?"

It was his turn to show disgust.

Being sightless (and often clueless), worms made poor informants. They were unreliable, always worried about mating or claws ripping them from the moist belly of the earth. So police usually dismissed them.

*

THE LAB WAS DESERTED as I oozed my way in, late afternoon. The fading light did not hinder my search. A wide pattern of scents, cloying, earthy, organic, illuminated the chamber. A row of elderberry roots defined the examination space.

The odorless space was vacant.

Glam's desiccated body had been disposed of by grateful bugs. There was nothing to be gained by further analysis, the tech had said.

But I did not agree. I took the evidence bag from the stone shelf and tucked it under my mantle.

As I turned, I became aware of a strong pheromone message. The tech guy was waiting near the entrance.

"Doing overtime, officer?" he signed.

I rippled slowly to exit the premise without squishing the bag. Alas, the tech had other ideas in mind.

"There's a rain forecast for tonight," the tech signed, rippling languorously toward me. "You should stay in."

I didn't care for his patronizing tone. As if I was too stupid to read the current moisture level!

He didn't get my refusal message. Worse, he made the first mating gesture, straining his head and torso up, up, until he almost touched the roof.

"After all, it's spring," he signed with a devious stench.

His posturing didn't impress me, but I needed to get out without giving away my theft. So I matched his moves, stretching my own head up (but not all the way up, mind you).

My response sent him giggling. I smelled all the nuances of his desire.

"I knew you would not resist a true semen bearer," the tech signaled as his left aperture opened. A silver dart protruded from a build-up of slime on his flank.

I squeezed through, the dart striking my shell in the process. Another battle scratch, I thought as I undulated out of reach of his drooling mouth.

But the shame followed in my slime.

*

I ONCE HAD BEEN YOUNG and light-footed. At a composter's feast, I spotted a handsome two-cycler, his shell striped with intricate dark, medium and light patterns.

His scent, combined with the yeast coating his shell, conspired to make me fall shell over foot for him.

We eloped from the crowd and mated under a generous cabbage.

After a long slobbering kiss, I sent my love dart. As did my partner. The mutual piercing brought us to ecstasy.

Alas, in the middle of the mating frenzy, my penis got stuck. No way to retire from my mate's aperture. It had to be ripped off.

Afterwards, I could only mate as a female.

This traumatic event altered my hermo friends and colleagues' attitudes. They began to treat me as less than equal, calling me "egg-sack", as if the only thing I could do was carry eggs.

With luck and lots of effort, I developed my skills at sniffing out liars, doing the odd job for the Police.

One mid-dawn, an investigator got accidentally crushed by a giant's foot. I was called upon to help with the unfinished case. It wasn't a big case, but that was how I got Zgouish as a partner.

*

LIGHTNING FLASHES STRIPED the late afternoon sky, their delayed vibrations rattling my shell. Soon, fat drops of rain splattered on the ground.

Tucked inside my shell, I waited on the exposed slab near the tomatoes' stand.

I did not fear predators. As raindrops exploded on the landscape, I knew most deathclaws would be safely tucked under the branches, in their twiggy nests or burrowed in holes.

Soon, the subterranean inhabitants broke through the soggy soil, fleeing their fast-filling galleries.

Sloggers were good at sniffing crime, but worms were endowed with the best sense of smell in all Garden districts.

Problem was, this incredible sense was too specialized. As clods and grains of sand passed their digestive tract, their smell was attuned to the mineral rather than the organic.

However, worms were active burrowers, processing tons of earth. I stretched out of my shell, upper stalks waving water off my eyes.

Here, you smell this, I exhaled in mucous scents.

The trick with dumb informants was to use the right incentive. So a few grains of calcium-rich dolomite, along with the remnants of the deceased in the evidence bag, proved to be a tempting reward.

Soon, I had pumped a dozen worms for tips, none of those useful. (Did I really care about which half of Tom number one would end up copulating with Nan, and how were they related?)

Then, a very fat earthworm curved its annulated body around my shell. The bigger were the more experienced. The old worm sniffed the residue in the bag, gobbling up my last dolomite grains in the process.

I smelled this near Basement, he exhaled.

Did I pick the right scent?

"Repeat, and directions," I asked.

The big worm complied.

Basement, west wall window.

I let the worm have the rest of the bag.

*

YOU HAD TO CROSS A HARD BRIDGE, then ooze through a hole in the flat transparent window.

Once inside, Basement offered a paradise: heat, moisture, darkness, water puddles, and rich food in boxes, bottles, silver cans, cardboard boxes. Of course, this meant that Basement was home to a wide variety of Garden's less savory elements. Well-behaved sloggers avoided the district.

I crawled vertically down the inner window sill, until I reached a wooden stair. Then I slogged down, passing a sweet-smelling silver cylinder lying against the wall.

A lot of sloggers were feasting on the premises.

Slugs, shell-less and shameless, were omnipresent, their stinky trails crisscrossing the cement. As were the ants, roaches, centipedes, hoping to get some crumbs.

Most lived there, despite the accrued risk. But in the night, the giants retired to their own, mountainous burrows over Basement.

I smelled aster pods, mammal's urine, granite and dolomite dust, rotten fruits, all dominated by an enticing aroma which was Basement's main appeal.

Liquid, honeyed yeast.

I did not have Zgouish's keen eyesight, but I could guess tall bottles jutting up from cardboard box. Brown bottles lay on the cement. Sliming closer, I discovered intoxicated sloggers absorbing the golden puddles of yeast inside.

A slick buck called out from a fallen bottle's entrance. His unmarked shell sported vivid purple and orange stripes.

"Hey babe, wanna mix some fluid?" he signed.

Despite the yeast aroma tugging at me, I chose to ignore him. The flashy buck sent an olfactive expletive as I crossed his slime path.

As I oozed my way deeper in Basement, I got more slug-calls. I was tempted to call the Chief for support.

However, such a course of action would give him proof of typical egg-sack unreliability. If it wasn't for my uncanny talent, he would have retired me from active duty and put me behind a leaf.

*

I HAD ELECTED TO AVOID the smelliest crowd near an upturned potato sack. More bottles were lying around.

A strong odor of formic acid alerted me.

A hapless, medium-sized earthworm was slowly devoured by a bunch of brown and red ants. It was dead, but its struggling body didn't know it yet. The ants didn't care, each taking a small bite and walking back to the entrance I used.

That sorry sight took too much of my attention. I almost swooped inside my shell when a nasty olfactive curse exploded nearby.

"We don't like to have police worms meddling in our affairs."

Without moving my foot, I twisted my upper body and one eyestalk.

They had slimed into a half circle, two sloggers, one big with a scarred shell, the other a first-cycler, his shell still unmarked. Three slugs cut my escape path to the window. Their stench almost gagged me.

"I want to speak to Glam's friends," I emitted, hoping my Glam olfactive signature was accurate.

Being those ants' next meal wasn't on my career trail.

"Glam's a good buddy," the biggest thug emitted.

"We would follow his trail everywhere," the smaller slogger said.

"Even if it means getting killed like him?"

The group smelled surprised.

"What do you mean, getting killed?" the first-cycler signed. "We were told he had slimed away!"

"Really? And who gave you that piece of news?"

"It's—"

The slogger did not finish his sentence. A purple and orange mass drove on him, upsetting his shell and forcing his eyestalks to withdraw inside his head. His sweat glands went bozo.

A new, arrogant scent message rose.

"Don't sweat too much, little egg."

The flashy-shelled buck from the bottle trashed the first-cycler, until the latter retracted inside his shell.

Then, the flashy buck turned his eyestalks to me.

"Fancy that, an egg-sack coming to smell dirt in our turf!" he said, advancing toward me.

This flashy thug didn't impress me.

I wasn't a first-cycler fresh from the egg, but a three-cycler, battle-trained. I had a specially-built defensive froth of mucus ready for those occasions.

Nevertheless, sliming over six opponents would exhaust my resources. So I plodded straight on.

"Speaking of dirt, what do you know about Melizz?" I said, putting an acidic scorn in my question.

The big, scarred thug rolled an eye at Flashy.

I cast a glance to the first-cycler who had seemed so eager to talk. He was hastily cementing his epiphragm shut. No way I could sniff out the truth from him. He must have been really frightened, which meant I was sliming closer to the bottom of this case.

Flashy moved so our shells blocked his buddies' sight.

He stretched his head, his stalks moving up and down, the first move of a mating ritual. His unmarked shell was deceiving: his ease betrayed a long experience.

"So, sweet gunk? It's mid-spring, you know?"

"I'm searching for Melizz," I said, ignoring his come-on line. "You may have crossed his trail."

"And what if I did?" Flashy signed, rippling on.

"Melizz has gone into hiding," I replied, oozing back to prevent him getting close. "Glam must have helped him to a stash of solid yeast, somewhere in Garden."

Solid yeast, a high-value currency among the Basement gangs, was a plausible murder motive.

"Solid yeast? If there was some here, we would have heard of it."

His lateral aperture irised open as he talked. Flashy had positioned himself so that his vulgar love dart would pierce my skin. I slogged sideways.

"You seem to know a lot about yeast traffic," I signed.

His released dart sailed into empty air.

"You're feisty for an egg-sack," he signed back.

My shell bumped on something. I looked back, keeping my other eyestalk on Flashy.

Semi-transparent brown bottles were lying around. One of those had a sizable portion of beer inside. A cloyed honeyed scent was wafting out the opened neck.

The ring of his buddies had reformed, pushing my shell toward the opening.

The situation was hopeless. Flashy and his gang could force me inside the bottle. Then, they could either seal the entrance with mucus and let me drown in the fumes, or use the occasion to mate.

I expelled a first wave of defensive mucus, catching Flashy in the side.

"You're just not helping, sweety gunk!" he snarled.

I stuck to my ground, sweating profusely. But before my glued foot could stick, the vulgar slugs gobbled up my slime faster than I could emit it.

The scarred thug sent me rolling sideways, Flashy emitting a strong scent of amusement.

Just as they were pushing me across the threshold, a familiar smell mingled in, sending a powerful pheromone command.

"GGPD! *Freeze!*"

*

ZGOUISH HAD ANGLED HIS MASSIVE BODY to ooze past two gang members, trailing over a smaller slug. The other slugs slimed away, past the now-lifeless earthworm.

My partner fell on the scarred thug, biting and spurting mucus, along with multiple olfactive expletives. The thug was heavier, but Zgouish's combat skills were unmatched in Garden.

Their slugfest ended when my partner forced the thug back inside his shell.

Flashy tried to escape by sliming along the bottle. I sent a burst of glue mucus. The slick slogger's foot congealed on the spot. His shell, still moving, struck the brown glass.

"Take us to Melizz," I ordered.

"You will never find him," Flashy replied.

The bottle rolled away, crashing against another.

"Eastern Wall, near the Ivy root," a tiny scent wafted.

It came from the closed shell of the first-cycler, where a small hole had been pierced.

*

ZGOUISH AND I TRAILED BACK to the window. We had been light on Flashy and his gang. In turn, they confirmed Glam had smelled happy, giving away yeast grains.

"It was courageous of you to come to Basement," I signed. "How did you know?"

"A big bad worm told me."

"You talk to worms, now?" I signed, emitting a flash of amusement.

"After the Mouse case was closed, I followed your trail."

We reached the ledge with the silver cylinder. As we trailed past the recipient, Basement's moonlight hues were replaced by a white light, brilliant as the sun.

A concert of panic scents filled the air.

Vibrations shook the wooden stairs. A formidable shadow obscured the blinding light.

From my position on the ledge, I saw in a daze the giant's monstrous legs stomping the cement floor, the big boot soles crushing shells. Panic emissions sank into nothingness and blood smells.

The air itself was trembling with a vibration my lower stalks could not decipher. Like rabbits and mice, giants wore air receptors. So they had emitters, somewhere.

An urgent smell shook me from my morbid fascination. "In here!" Zgouish said.

He was oozing across the round door of the silver can, his big shell rubbing the edges. I hastened inside. The can was half-filled with a syrupy liquid. Honeyed yeast.

A lone ant was slurping the beer. It scurried away.

As we moved inside, the can rolled off the ledge, catapulting us one against the other. We retracted in our shells, bouncing around.

Our can was lifted up. It swung, to and fro, the puddle of beer swooshing around us. I glued myself to the metal, grateful it wasn't copper.

Basement scents fell away so fast it was dizzying.

The swinging stopped.

Suddenly, Zgouish and I found ourselves weightless, a sensation playing havoc with our statocysts. The can had been dropped from a great height.

Weight returned with a vengeance as our can landed abruptly. The jolt unglued me from the curved floor and sent me against the opening.

A harsh, unnatural blue wall surrounded our can, suffusing me with plastic scent.

I slimed down to the beer puddle at the bottom of the can. Zgouish and I were unharmed, of course: the silver metal shell had protected us.

"Where are we?" I enquired, my foot sucking up more than a few drops of liquid yeast.

"Back Door Area."

The worst place, ever.

"Inside."

Better and better.

"We're lost," I signed.

"There's a way out. At mid-dawn, giants bring this big blue box near the North Grey Plain. But we have to wait until then."

The can shifted, pulling our shells together.

"Gowoon. We could put that time to good use," Zgouish signed. "It's spring, after all."

"That's beer-talking," I said, aware of his scent.

But the ambient heat and the beer fumes conspired against me. I felt like sliding down a funnel of desire.

"You know I can't...reciprocate," I replied, weakly.

"I don't give a clod what you were before, or what you are now," Zgouish signalled.

The yeast must be going to my brain, I thought.

"I would bathe into your slime, Gowoon," he signed, his sweat truthful.

His sincere oath had me oozing and sweating all over.

I won't linger over the passionate exchange of fluids that followed. Suffice to say that if the Chief ever learned of this mating, my chances to make the Hall of Gastropod Fame would quickly evaporate.

*

As Zgouish had surmised, at mid-dawn, a giant carried the box at the northern reaches of Garden. It took the rest of mid-dawn to extricate ourselves from the silver can, escalate the blue plastic wall and slime down among tall blades of grass.

The grass parted to reveal the Northern Gray Plain, so vast my eyestalks could not see the other side.

"There is another side," Zgouish said, stretching both eyestalks parallel.

I envied his sight; I could only guess at the spot where we found Thumper.

The fresh air cleared the beer fumes from our brains.

We decided not to tell anyone about our tryst. Inside me, I felt the first delicate stirring of new eggs forming.

Well, it was spring after all.

*

It had rained that night, and we replenished our water reserves en route. We had to cross the damp grass, then creep along a flat white slab, one of many composing a deadly route along the eastern wall.

Giants and their black soles used it often, but the crevices between the slabs were safe paths.

Of course, when we slogged to the gnarled ivy root going up the eastern wall, there was no Melizz in view. Nothing but moist ivy leaves and spicy crumbs of aster pods.

"I hate junk food," I said.

The wind brought a strong, honeyed scent.

"There," Zgouish said.

It was Melizz, munching an aster pod. I recognized his striped shell.

"GGPD! *Freeze!*" I ordered, hoping that my powerful emission would compensate for my lack of command pheromones.

Our quarry did not heed me. He slimed up the wall, followed by Zgouish.

I sucked it up and went after them.

Element of the case joined together like mucus globs: Glam too generous in Basement; his friends talking too much, sleazy Melizz following Glam to get the stash. Killing Glam, in mid morning, then leaving his body on the sun-exposed rock so every clue would have evaporated by afternoon.

Melizz was slowing down. Zgouish gained on him, his athlete's body flowing at the speed of lightning.

Suddenly, I slipped down.

Normally I loved water, but the wall's vegetation was dripping all over us, making climbing a chore. Scents were attenuated; I barely smelled Zgouish's expletives as he almost lost his foot grip, high over me.

But we slogged on. An angry wasp buzzed by, two yeast grains in its clutches.

Suddenly I spotted a flash of metal.

At the same time, an aroma of joy reached me, Zgouish's victory message.

"The stash!"

As I made my way up, I could smell the powerful, concentrated yeast scent. I trailed closer. An addled giant had stuck a can in the vines, several stems supporting it.

The can lay sideways, so rain did not seep in by its hole. Evaporation had turned the golden liquid into a sticky mud, easy to mold into balls and pass around at Basement feasts.

This was the treasure trove worth killing for.

Between the leaves, I saw Melizz creep inside the can, as to trap my partner inside.

Instead of following the perp, Zgouish crept between the bricks and the metal. I lost sight of him.

Then Melizz sent an acidic fear call. *You can't do that!*

Another call: *Watch me!*

A wasp flashed out of the hole as the support stems bent more. Zgouish was stretching his body and pushing against the metal. One stem gave out and broke. Then the whole can rolled off the other stems, tumbling down past me.

Zgouish! I sent, worry grabbing my insides.

A scented call came, deteriorated by the wind.

Don't sweat! Melizz landed on the slab.

I looked down, trusting my partner's keen eyesight.

The height was dizzying, but I could make out a brown smudge, and the can shining on the slab. A medium-hued blob was extracting itself from the container.

Sliming down would take me too long. I took a desperate gamble. I pulled in my eyes and retreated inside my shell.

Then I let go of the wall.

*

MY FALL WAS MERCIFULLY SHORT. I rebounded on the soft earth band between the slab and the wall.

Extending an eyestalk, I saw the top of Melizz's shell as he strove to reach the eastern fence.

A high wooden barrier overgrown by weeds marked the limit of our jurisdiction. There was a passage under, mid-slab. Melizz would go straight for the hole, while I would slog around the slab's right angles.

The thought of that murderer escaping scot-free contracted my resolve. I drew more water from my reserves. Risky for my eggs, but duty passed first.

Instead of following the passage, I slimed up to the slab surface. Then, I hurried after his receding silhouette.

Melizz was quick, but I was trained. I couldn't believe the lightning rate of my progress on this smooth surface. I began to angle my trail to intercept him. With each wave, the suspect's shell became more and more clearly delineated, until I could distinguish yeast grains sticking to his shell.

Then everything went south.

Mounting vibrations, low-frequency but strong, alerted me.

Giant, coming fast! I sent.

I unstuck my foot from the slab and retracted into my shell, instants before an approaching vibration sent me rolling. When my shell stopped moving, I opened an eyestalk.

A huge shadow loomed over the slab.

Melizz saw it too late.

A dark wall smelling of moist earth stomped his last burst of fear. The wall stood there, its smooth surface a mineral green. I prepared myself for a fast squishing death.

Then the wall disappeared.

I turned my eyestalks to glimpse the giant receding north, already incredibly far over the horizon.

A silver can shone in one immense paw.

Of Melizz, nothing recognizable was left. Fragments of his shell were spread in a wide circle. Brown yeast powder rose, tempting, then it was scattered by the wind.

*

ZGOUISH AND I WERE SLOGGING towards the GGPD head-quarters. We took our sweet time, talking and eating.

"Zgouish, how can you see so far?" I asked, munching on a small strawberry.

He waved his eyestalks in a parallel line.

"It's a trick. I direct my two eyestalks toward the same point, adding them up in my brain. It gives a better image."

"Amazing! You should talk to the Chief."

Zgouish gave me his attractive bad-slogger shrug.

"What, so he could work me to death? I'd rather keep him thinking I'm just a bunch of muscles!"

"Well, you're that, too," I replied, letting a tang of teasing creep in my scent.

I felt light-footed and light-headed. Must be the beer.

But, after all, it *was* spring.

THE END

Heartfelt Thanks

Slime & Crime has been originally published in Fiction River 22, 2017, edited by WMG Publishing inc. under the direction of John Helfers.

If you enjoyed this story, share your impressions on your favorite platform! This way, you gently guide more readers towards Michèle's stories.

About the Author

WHEN NOT TRYING to initiate first contact with strange flora, Michèle Laframboise juggles her time between drawing comics and crafting stories.

A science-fiction lover since childhood, she has published 17 novels and more than 40 short stories, earning three Auroras and two Solaris awards.

Her works have appeared in *Solaris, Carmilla, Galaxies, Géante Rouge, Brin d'Éternité, Tesseracts, Fiction River, Compelling Science Fiction*, and *Abyss&Apex*. She has been translated into French, Italian and Russian.

Holding degrees in geography and engineering, Michèle uses her scientific background to create worlds filled with humor, invention and wonder.

Official website:
www.michele-laframboise.com
in French and English

Humoristic blog:
sundayartist.wordpress.com

Publisher's website:
www.echofictions.com

Wikipedia entry: Michèle Laframboise

For some news and amusing reading reviews, join
 Michele's happy band of readers!

http://michele-laframboise.com/fans

Other books by Michèle

Change or die!

Science-fiction / humor / First contact

Loongunis need constant fluctuations to thrive, while the strange-haired Earthmen hate the endless instability.

When a sabotage impairs the shift engines of their traveling Box, the enforced immobility might drive all Loongunis mad...unless their translator can work out a solution!

Science fiction adventure at its best, a quirky 7000-word story told by multiple award-winning author Michèle Laframboise.

How to Think inside the Box
978-1-988339-40-5 (print)

Trapped in the most beautiful place on earth...

Humor / mystery / Ornithology

Equipped with her Sibley Guide and trusty binoculars, Amanda Byrd pursues the most elusive winged species. As she explores a beautiful canyon at dawn, Amanda discovers their lift sabotaged, trapping their group at the canyon's bottom.

Who did it, and why?

Our intrepid birdwatcher must find a way out before the sun turns the canyon into a mortal cauldron.

A short and spirited cozy mystery introducing the energetic Lady Byrd, written by Michèle Laframboise, multi-award winner author and amateur ornithologist.

Condor Cliff

ISBN 978-1-988339-08-5 (Print)

You won't forget Malak...

Child Labor/ Humanitarian / Sweatshops

Theo, a dispirited workplace humanitarian, audits a child

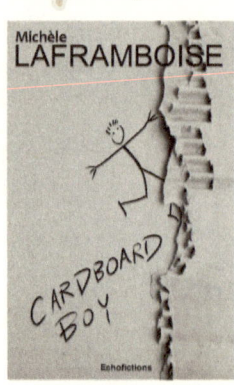

worker at a cardboard factory, in a port city somewhere in Asia. He is impressed by young Malak's maturity and grit. When that boy, the same age as Theo's own son, disappears, he cannot let it rest. His quest for answers only raises more questions about the traps of structured help and acquired privilege.

An unsettling story quietly told by multiple awards-winning author Michèle Laframboise.

Cardboard Boy

ISBN 978-1-988339-22-1 (Print)

More on Echofictions.com/books

Friends' List

A story links every reader in a chain of friendship. Feel free to write your name before you give this book to someone close.

This is a unique feature of the printed edition!

_____

_____

_____

_____

_____

_____

_____

_____

_____

_____

Yearning for more Stories?

Michèle Laframboise's full bibliography is enough to whet any reader's appetite! Visit her author site at:
michele-laframboise.com

New stories are brewing up constantly!

To get exclusive offers, curated book reviews, advanced information on events, join Michele's happy band of readers!

michele-laframboise.com/fans

As a very busy writer, Michèle won't send mail more often than once every two months.

www.ingramcontent.com/pod-product-compliance
Lightning Source LLC
Chambersburg PA
CBHW020607130626
46552CB00007B/3089